The Crab
that played
with the Sea

Rudyard Kipling

Illustrated by Michael Foreman

PETER BEDRICK BOOKS
NEW YORK

First American edition published in 1983 by Peter
Bedrick Books. Published by agreement with Mac-
millan Children's Books, a division of Macmillan
Publishers Ltd., London and Basingstoke.

Library of Congress Cataloging-in-Publication Data
Kipling, Rudyard, 1865–1936.
   The crab that played with the sea.

   Summary: Relates how the crab came to live both
in the sea and on land and to lose its hard shell once
a year.
   [1. Crabs—Fiction] I. Foreman, Michael, 1938–
ill. II. Title.
PZ7.K632Cr   1983   [Fic]   83-71484
ISBN 0-911745-06-8

Second printing, 1986
Printed in Hong Kong
Reinforced binding

Distributed in the USA by Harper & Row

BEFORE the High and Far-Off Times, O my Best Beloved, came the Time of the Very Beginnings; and that was in the days when the Eldest Magician was getting Things ready. First he got the Earth ready; then he got the Sea ready; and then he told all the Animals that they could come out and play. And the Animals said, 'O Eldest Magician, what shall we play at?' and he said, 'I will show you.' He took the Elephant —All-the-Elephant-there-was—and said, 'Play at being an Elephant,' and All-the-Elephant-there-was played. He took the Beaver—all-the-Beaver-there-was—and said, 'Play at being a Beaver,' and All-the-Beaver-there-was played. He took the Cow—All-the-Cow-there-was —and said, 'Play at being a Cow,' and All-the-Cow-there-was played. He took the Turtle—All-the-Turtle-there-was—and said, 'Play at being a Turtle,' and All-the-Turtle-there-was played. One by one he took all the beasts and birds and fishes and told them what to play at.

3

But towards evening, when people and things grow restless and tired, there came up the Man (With his own little girl-daughter?)—Yes, with his own best-beloved little girl-daughter sitting upon his shoulder, and he said, 'What is this play, Eldest Magician?' And the Eldest Magician said, 'Ho! Son of Adam, this is the play of the Very Beginning; but you are too wise for this play.' And the Man saluted and said, 'Yes, I am too wise for this play; but see that you make all the Animals obedient to me.'

Now, while the two were talking together, Pau Amma the Crab, who was next in the game, scuttled off sideways and stepped into the sea, saying to himself, 'I will play my play alone in the deep waters, and I will never be obedient to this son of Adam.' Nobody saw him go away except the little girl-daughter where she leaned on the Man's shoulder. And the play went on till there were no more Animals left without orders; and the Eldest Magician wiped the fine dust off his hands and walked about the world to see how the Animals were playing.

He went North, Best Beloved, and he found All-the-Elephant-there-was digging with his tusks and stamping with his feet in the nice new clean earth that had been made ready for him.

'Kun?' said All-the-Elephant-there-was, meaning, 'Is this right?'

'Payah kun,' said the Eldest Magician, meaning, 'That is quite right'; and he breathed upon the great rocks and lumps of earth that All-the-Elephant-there-was had

thrown up, and they became the great Himalayan Mountains, and you can look them out on the map.

He went East, and he found All-the-Cow-there-was feeding in the field that had been made ready for her, and she licked her tongue round a whole forest at a time, and swallowed it and sat down to chew her cud.

'*Kun?*' said All-the-Cow-there-was.

'*Payah kun,*' said the Eldest Magician; and he breathed upon the bare patch where she had eaten, and upon the place where she had sat down, and one became the great Indian Desert, and the other became the Desert of Sahara, and you can look them out on the map.

6

He went West, and he found All-the-Beaver-there-was making a beaver-dam across the mouths of broad rivers that had been got ready for him.

'*Kun?*' said All-the-Beaver-there-was.

'*Payah kun,*' said the Eldest Magician; and he breathed upon the fallen trees and the still water, and they became the Everglades in Florida, and you may look them out on the map.

Then he went South and found All-the-Turtle-there-was scratching with his flippers in the sand that had been got ready for him, and the sand and the rocks whirled through the air and fell far off into the sea.

7

'*Kun?*' said All-the-Turtle-there-was.

'*Payah kun,*' said the Eldest Magician; and he breathed upon the sand and the rocks, where they had fallen in the sea, and they became the most beautiful islands of Borneo, Celebes, Sumatra, Java, and the rest of the Malay Archipelago, and you can look *them* out on the map!

By and by the Eldest Magician met the Man on the banks of the Perak River, and said, 'Ho! Son of Adam, are all the Animals obedient to you?'

'Yes,' said the Man.

'Is all the Earth obedient to you?'

8

'Yes,' said the Man.

'Is all the Sea obedient to you?'

'No,' said the Man. 'Once a day and once a night the Sea runs up the Perak River and drives the sweet water back into the forest, so that my house is made wet; once a day and once a night it runs down the river and draws all the water after it, so that there is nothing left but mud, and my canoe is upset. Is that the play you told it to play?'

'No,' said the Eldest Magician. 'That is a new and a bad play.'

'Look!' said the Man, and as he spoke the great Sea came up the mouth of the Perak River, driving the river backwards till it overflowed all the dark forests for miles and miles, and flooded the Man's house.

'This is wrong. Launch your canoe and we will find out who is playing with the Sea,' said the Eldest Magician. They stepped into the canoe; the little girl-daughter came with them; and the Man took his *kris*—a curving, wavy dagger with a blade like a flame,—and they pushed out on the Perak River. Then the Sea began to run back and back, and the canoe was sucked out of the mouth of the Perak River, past Selangor, past Malacca, past Singapore, out and out to the Island of Bintang, as though it had been pulled by a string.

Then the Eldest Magician stood up and shouted, 'Ho! beasts, birds, and fishes, that I took between my hands at the Very Beginning and taught the play that you should play, which one of you is playing with the Sea?'

9

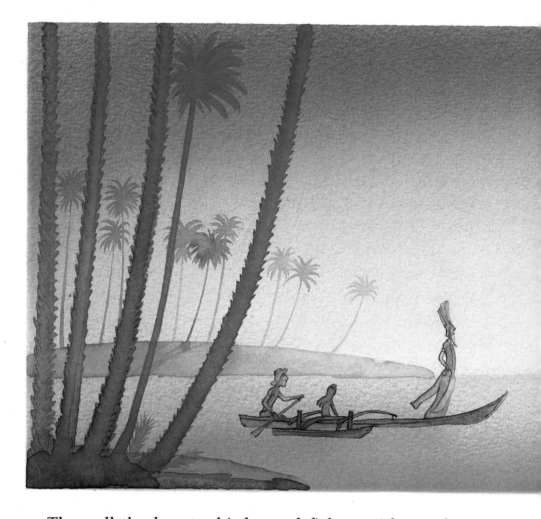

Then all the beasts, birds, and fishes said together, 'Eldest Magician, we play the plays that you taught us to play—we and our children's children. But not one of us plays with the Sea.'

Then the Moon rose big and full over the water, and the Eldest Magician said to the hunchbacked old man who sits in the Moon spinning a fishing-line with which he hopes one day to catch the World, 'Ho! Fisher of the

Moon, are you playing with the Sea?'

'No,' said the Fisherman, 'I am spinning a line with which I shall some day catch the World; but I do not play with the Sea.' And he went on spinning his line.

Now there is also a Rat up in the Moon who always bites the old Fisherman's line as fast as it is made, and the Eldest Magician said to him, 'Ho! Rat of the Moon, are *you* playing with the Sea?'

And the Rat said, 'I am too busy biting through the line that this old Fisherman is spinning. I do not play with the Sea.' And he went on biting the line.

Then the little girl-daughter put up her little soft brown arms with the beautiful white shell bracelets and said, 'O Eldest Magician! when my father here talked to you at the Very Beginning, and I leaned upon his shoulder while the beasts were being taught their plays, one beast went away naughtily into the Sea before you had taught him his play.'

And the Eldest Magician said, 'How wise are little children who see and are silent! What was that beast like?'

And the little girl-daughter said, 'He was round and he was flat; and his eyes grew upon stalks; and he walked sideways like this; and he was covered with strong armour upon his back.'

And the Eldest Magician said, 'How wise are little children who speak truth! Now I know where Pau Amma went. Give me the paddle!'

So he took the paddle; but there was no need to paddle, for the water flowed steadily past all the islands till they came to the place called Pusat Tasek—the Heart of the Sea—where the great hollow is that leads down to the heart of the world, and in that hollow grows the Wonderful Tree, Pauh Janggi, that bears the magic twin-

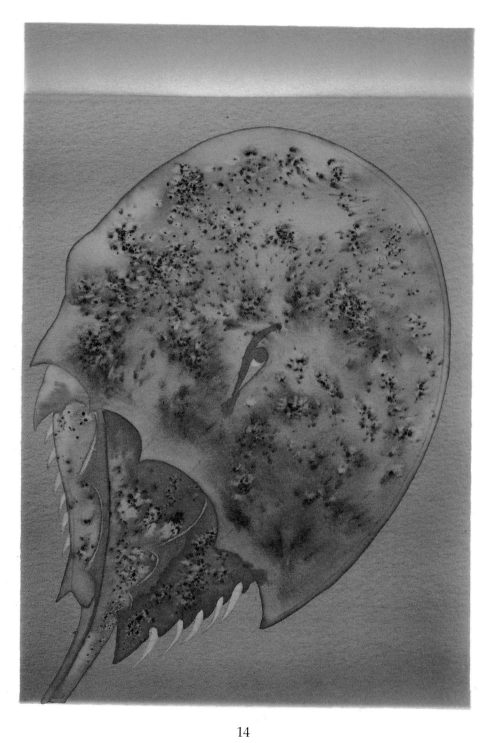

14

nuts. Then the Eldest Magician slid his arm up to the shoulder through the deep warm water, and under the roots of the Wonderful Tree he touched the broad back of Pau Amma the Crab. And Pau Amma settled down at the touch, and all the Sea rose up as water rises in a basin when you put your hand into it.

'Ah!' said the Eldest Magician. 'Now I know who has been playing with the Sea'; and he called out, 'What are you doing, Pau Amma?'

And Pau Amma, deep down below, answered, 'Once a day and once a night I go out to look for my food. Once a day and once a night I return. Leave me alone.'

Then the Eldest Magician said, 'Listen, Pau Amma. When you go out from your cave the waters of the Sea pour down into Pusat Tasek, and all the beaches of all the islands are left bare, and the little fish die, and Rajah Moyang Kaban, the King of the Elephants, his legs are made muddy. When you come back and sit in Pusat Tasek, the waters of the Sea rise, and half the little islands are drowned, and the Man's house is flooded, and Rajah Abdullah, the King of the Crocodiles, his mouth is filled with the salt water.'

Then Pau Amma, deep down below, laughed and said, 'I did not know I was so important. Henceforward I will go out seven times a day, and the waters shall never be still.'

And the Eldest Magician said, 'I cannot make you play the play you were meant to play, Pau Amma, because you escaped me at the Very Beginning; but if you are not afraid, come up and we will talk about it.'

'I am not afraid,' said Pau Amma, and he rose to the

top of the Sea in the moonlight. There was nobody in the world so big as Pau Amma—for he was the King Crab of all Crabs. Not a common Crab, but a King Crab. One

17

side of his great shell touched the beach at Sarawak; the other touched the beach at Pahang; and he was taller than the smoke of three volcanoes! As he rose up through the branches of the Wonderful Tree he tore off one of the great twin-fruits—the magic double-kernelled nuts that make people young,—and the little girl-daughter saw it bobbing alongside the canoe, and pulled it in and began to pick out the soft eyes of it with her little golden scissors.

'Now,' said the Magician, 'make a Magic, Pau Amma, to show that you are really important.'

Pau Amma rolled his eyes and waved his legs, but he could only stir up the Sea, because, though he was a King Crab, he was nothing more than a Crab, and the Eldest Magician laughed.

'You are not so important after all, Pau Amma,' he said. 'Now, let *me* try,' and he made a Magic with his left hand—with just the little finger of his left hand—and—lo and behold, Best Beloved, Pau Amma's hard, blue-green-black shell fell off him as a husk falls off a coconut, and Pau Amma was left all soft—soft as the little crabs that you sometimes find on the beach, Best Beloved.

'Indeed, you are very important,' said the Eldest Magician. 'Shall I ask the Man here to cut you with his *kris*? Shall I send for Rajah Moyang Kaban, the King of the Elephants, to pierce you with his tusks? or shall I call Rajah Abdullah, the King of the Crocodiles, to bite you?'

And Pau Amma said, 'I am ashamed! Give me back my hard shell and let me go back to Pusat Tasek, and I

18

will only stir out once a day and once a night to get my food.'

And the Eldest Magician said, 'No, Pau Amma, I will *not* give you back your shell, for you will grow bigger and prouder and stronger, and perhaps you will forget your promise, and you will play with the Sea once more.'

Then Pau Amma said, 'What shall I do? I am so big that I can only hide in Pusat Tasek, and if I go anywhere else, all soft as I am now, the sharks and the dogfish will eat me. And if I go to Pusat Tasek, all soft as I am now, though I may be safe, I can never stir out to get my food, and so I shall die.' Then he waved his legs and lamented.

'Listen, Pau Amma,' said the Eldest Magician. 'I cannot make you play the play you were meant to play, because you escaped me at the Very Beginning; but if you choose, I can make every stone and every hole and every bunch of weed in all the seas a safe Pusat Tasek for you and your children for always.'

Then Pau Amma said, 'That is good, but I do not choose yet. Look! there is that Man who talked to you at the Very Beginning. If he had not taken up your attention I should not have grown tired of waiting and run away, and all this would never have happened. What will *he* do for me?'

And the Man said, 'If you choose, I will make a Magic, so that both the deep water and the dry ground will be a home for you and your children—so that you shall be able to hide both on the land and in the sea.'

And Pau Amma said, 'I do not choose yet. Look! there is that girl who saw me running away at the Very Beginning. If she had spoken then, the Eldest Magician would have called me back, and all this would never have happened. What will *she* do for me?'

And the little girl-daughter said, 'This is a good nut that I am eating. If you choose, I will make a Magic and I will give you this pair of scissors, very sharp and strong, so that you and your children can eat coconuts like this all day long when you come up from the Sea to the land; or you can dig a Pusat Tasek for yourself with the scissors that belong to you when there is no stone or hole near by; and when the earth is too hard, by the help of these same scissors you can run up a tree.'

And Pau Amma said, 'I do not choose yet, for, all soft as I am, these gifts would not help me. Give me back my shell, O Eldest Magician, and then I will play your play.'

And the Eldest Magician said, 'I will give it back, Pau Amma, for eleven months of the year; but on the twelfth month of every year it shall grow soft again, to remind you and all your children that I can make Magics, and to keep you humble, Pau Amma; for I see that if you can run both under the water and on land, you will grow too bold; and if you can climb trees and crack nuts and dig holes with your scissors, you will grow too greedy, Pau Amma.'

Then Pau Amma thought a little and said, 'I have made my choice. I will take all the gifts.'

Then the Eldest Magician made a Magic with the right hand, with all five fingers of his right hand, and lo and behold, Best Beloved, Pau Amma grew smaller and smaller and smaller, till at last there was only a little green crab swimming in the water alongside the canoe, crying in a very small voice, 'Give me the scissors!'

And the girl-daughter picked him up on the palm of her little brown hand, and sat him in the bottom of the canoe and gave him her scissors, and he waved them in his little arms, and opened them and shut them and snapped them, and said, 'I can eat nuts. I can crack shells. I can dig holes. I can climb trees. I can breathe in the dry air, and I can find a safe Pusat Tasek under every stone. I did not know I was so important. *Kun?* [Is this right?]'

'*Payah kun,*' said the Eldest Magician, and he laughed and gave him his blessing; and little Pau Amma scuttled

over the side of the canoe into the water; and he was so
tiny that he could have hidden under the shadow of a
dry leaf on land or of a dead shell at the bottom of the
sea.

'Was that well done?' said the Eldest Magician.

'Yes,' said the Man. 'But now we must go back to
Perak, and that is a weary way to paddle. If we had
waited till Pau Amma had gone out of Pusat Tasek and
come home, the water would have carried us there by
itself.'

'You are lazy,' said the Eldest Magician. 'So your

children shall be lazy. They shall be the laziest people in the world. They shall be called the Malazy—the lazy people'; and he held up his finger to the Moon and said, 'O Fisherman, here is this Man too lazy to row home. Pull his canoe home with your line, Fisherman.'

'No,' said the Man. 'If I am to be lazy all my days, let the Sea work for me twice a day for ever. That will save paddling.'

And the Eldest Magician laughed and said, '*Payah kun* [That is right].'

And the Rat of the Moon stopped biting the line; and
the Fisherman let his line down till it touched the Sea,
and he pulled the whole deep Sea along, past the Island

of Bintang, past Singapore, past Malacca, past Selangor,
till the canoe whirled into the mouth of the Perak River
again.

'*Kun?*' said the Fisherman of the Moon.

'*Payah kun,*' said the Eldest Magician. 'See now that you pull the Sea twice a day and twice a night for ever, so that the Malazy fishermen may be saved paddling. But be careful not to do it too hard, or I shall make a Magic on you as I did to Pau Amma.'

Then they all went up the Perak River and went to bed, Best Beloved.

Now listen and attend!

From that day to this the Moon has always pulled the Sea up and down and made what we call the tides. Sometimes the Fisher of the Sea pulls a little too hard, and then we get spring-tides; and sometimes he pulls a little too softly, and then we get what are called neap-tides; but nearly always he is careful, because of the Eldest Magician.

And Pau Amma? You can see when you go to the beach, how all Pau Amma's babies make little Pusat Taseks for themselves under every stone and bunch of weed on the sands; you can see them waving their little scissors; and in some parts of the world they truly live on the dry land and run up the palm-trees and eat coconuts, exactly as the girl-daughter promised. But once a year all Pau Ammas must shake off their hard armour and be soft—to remind them of what the Eldest Magician could do. And so it isn't fair to kill or hunt Pau Amma's babies just because old Pau Amma was stupidly rude a very long time ago.

Oh yes! And Pau Amma's babies hate being taken out of their little Pusat Taseks and brought home in pickle-bottles. That is why they nip you with their scissors, and it serves you right!